Some of my good reviews:

'Will make you laugh out loud, cringe and snigger, all at the same time' -LoveReading4Kids

'WHAT'S NOT TO LOVE?' -Sun

'...and cheeky' -Booktictac, Guardian Online Review

Waterstones Children's Book Prize Shortlistee!

'The review of the eight year old boy in our house... "Can I keep it to give to a friend?" Best recommendation you can get' - Observer

'I LAUGHED SO MUCH, I THOUGHT THAT I WAS GOING TO BURST!' Finbar, aged 9

'HUGELY ENJOYABLE, SURREAL CHAOS' -Guardian

I am not~still~ a Loser The Roald Dahl FUNNY PRIZE WINNER 2013

EGMONT
We Bring Stories to Life

First published in Great Britain 2017
by Egmont UK Ltd, The Yellow Building,
1 Nicholas Road, London W11 4AN

Text and illustration copyright © Jim Smith 2017
The moral rights of Jim Smith have been asserted.

ISBN 978 1 4052 8397 7

barrylooser.com
www.egmont.co.uk

A CIP catalogue record for this title is available from
the British Library

Printed and bound in Great Britain by the CPI Group

63322/1

MIX
Paper
FSC® C013306

Barry Loser

and the birthday billions

upside down on purpose

From the squidgy pink brain of

Jim Smith

Barry's birthday

'Cock-a-doodle-dooooooo!' screeched
my baby brother, Desmond Loser the
Second, from his bedroom next to mine.

FLONK!

It was 6.17am on Saturday morning,
not that I minded because . . .

'IT'S MY BIRTHDAY!' I cried, jumping out of bed and running downstairs doing an excitement blowoff on every step.

'Happy birthday, my darling little Snookyflumps!' cooed my mum, cuddling me into her bright red fluffy dressing gown.

'Thanks Mumsy Wumsy!' I smiled, wriggling out of her cuddle and staring at the ginormous pile of presents sitting on our kitchen table.

In the middle of the pile sat a huge box covered in shiny silver paper.

that

'Fandabby-keelness*!' I cried, doing a bum-wiggle dance until my pyjama bottoms fell down.

*Keel = cool

I knew exactly what was inside the box - a SHNOZINATOR 9000!

I twizzled one of my eyeballs over to the present list I'd stuck on the fridge door nineteen and three-quarter weeks before.

It said:

1. Another yellow hoodie
2. No more boring questions about school
3. A SHNOZINATOR 9000!!!

My mum spotted me looking at the list. 'Ooh that reminds me,' she said. 'What did you do at school yesterday?'

'Erm . . . answer boring questions mostly,' I said, giving myself a mini salute for being so funny.

My mum did a face like a kangaroo eating a hedgehog and I dived into the presents, grabbing a squidgy jumperish-feeling one.*

fluffy red dressing gown

*I was saving the SHNOZINATOR 9000 till last.

'Hmmm . . . let me guess - a yellow hoodie?' I smiled, ripping it open. I'm famous for wearing yellow hoodies, in case you didn't know.

Inside the wrapping paper was a white polo neck jumper.

sorry for boring drawing

'Thought it'd make a change from all your yellow hoodies!' chuckled my dad.

all wrapped up like a pressie

'Plus it's just like the one Wolf Tizzler wears in his adverts!' said my mum, and I did a bday eye-roll because I'm comperleeterly bored of hearing my mum go on about Wolf Tizzler the whole time.

Er, who's Wolf Tizzler?

Wolf Tizzler is the annoying child genius who invented the 'ZOOM-E-BROOM', a new kind of broom with microscopic wheels on the ends of its bristles.

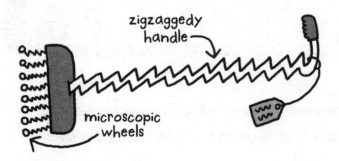

zigzaggedy handle

microscopic wheels

Wolf Tizzler's always on TV doing adverts about how the microscopic wheels are supposed to make the ZOOM-E-BROOM go faster when you're sweeping up.

Wolf Tizzler

I think my mum thinks Wolf Tizzler would be the most perfect son ever.

'Thanks Mum, thanks Dad,' I said, not that I really wanted a white polo neck jumper.

'Don't thank us, it's from Desmond!' said my dad.

To Barry
From Des
xxx

— except Des can't write

'Thanks Desmond,' I said, even though I knew there was no way my baby brother had gone into a Feeko's supermarket and bought me a Wolf Tizzler polo neck jumper all on his own.

I reached down and patted him on the head.

'Me got a biskit!' shouted Desmond, who was sitting on the floor with his bum squidged into a potty.

used to be mine

biscuit

He took a bite of the dinosaur-shaped biscuit he was holding. 'Me not want biskit!' he spluttered, spraying bits of biscuit all over the kitchen tiles.

'No probbles!' said my mum, grabbing her ZOOM-E-BROOM and sweeping the crumbs into a dustpan. 'Thanks to its microscopic bristle-wheel technology, the ZOOM-E-BROOM is up to ninety per cent faster than the next-fastest broom on the market!' she smiled.

like she's in an advert

'Isn't that what that Rolf Twizzler kid says in his adverts?' said my dad.

'Ooh, he's such a clever boy!' cooed my mum.

'I'm clever too!' I said, yanking my white polo neck over my head. 'Look - I can hardly get this jumper on what with my ginormous brain and everything!'

NNNGGGFFF!!!

'More like your ginormous nose!' chuckled my dad, even though his nose is WAY bigger than mine.

More rubbish pressies

After that I opened all my other presents - apart from the huge shiny silver one with the SHNOZINATOR 9000 inside. This is what I got . . .

1. A bright pink piggy bank from my Granny Harumpadunk:

imagine it's pink

2. Wolf Tizzler's autobiography, HOW TO BE A GENIUS LIKE ME, from my mum:

3. One of those build-your-own circuit board kits from my dad:

'Brillikeels,' I said, pretending I liked them all even though:

1. I don't have any money to put in a piggy bank

2. Who wants to read a boring old book about a loserish child genius who loves brooms?

3. There was no way I'd be wasting my time building a stupid circuit board when I had a SHNOZINATOR 9000 to play with!

The Shnozinator 9000

You're probably wondering what a SHNOZINATOR 9000 is by now. It's this keel new gaming helmet that makes you feel like you've been transported to Shnozville.

some loser

SHNOZ-INATOR 9000!

Shnozville is where **Future Ratboy** lives, by the way.

Future Ratboy is my favourite TV show. It's all about this keel kid who's been zapped millions of years into the future and transformed into a half-boy, half-rat, half-TV.

boy

rat

TV

'Oh. My. Keelness!' I said, ripping open
the huge shiny silver present. Inside
was a white cardboard box with
'SHNOZINATOR 9000' written on
it in futuristic letters.

'A SHNOZINATOR 9000! Thanks,
Mummypoos. Thanks, Daddypoos!'
I said, lifting it out of the box and
slotting it over my head.

Nothing happened.

visor slots
down

'Er, why in the unkeelness aren't I in
Shnozville?' I said, my nose beginning
to droop.

'You've got to charge it up first, Barry!'
chuckled my dad, pulling a mile-long
cable out of the box and plugging it
into the wall.

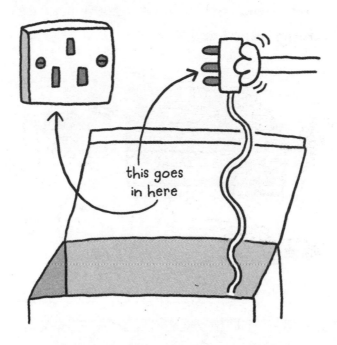

this goes
in here

'Oh yeah!' I said, and my mum did
a face that looked like she thought
Wolf Tizzler probably would've
worked that out.

I lifted the SHNOZINATOR 9000 off my head and plugged it into the other end of the cable and a little green triangle lit up on the side.

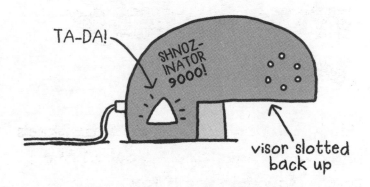

TA-DA!

SHNOZ-INATOR 9000!

visor slotted back up

'SHNOZINATOR 9000 CHARGING!' bleeped a robotty voice.

'Time for a bday wee!' I said, plonking the SHNOZINATOR 9000 down on the kitchen table and walking off all happily towards the toilet.

After I did my bday wee

'Ahhh, that's what I call a fantastikeels bday wee!' I said, strolling out of the toilet. 'Now, let's see if my SHNOZINATOR 9000's charged up!'

I walked into the kitchen and froze.

My SHNOZINATOR 9000 wasn't on the table where I'd left it. Instead, there was a trail of white electric cable stretching from the plug socket through the archway into the living room.

also known as 'sitting room'

I followed the cable into the living room and froze again.

'Waaahhh!' I screamed.

Desmond Loser the Second was sitting on the carpet in front of the telly, his bum squidged into my upside-down SHNOZINATOR 9000 like it was his potty.

He was watching his favourite TV show, Clowny Wowny, and his face was very red. Desmond's face being very red is never a good thing.

'Operation Get Desmond's Bum Out of My SHNOZINATOR 9000 Before He Does a Poo in It!' I screamed, flying through the air like **Future Ratboy**.

Future RatBarry GO!

I scooped Des out of the SHNOZINATOR 9000 and plonked him on the sofa then twizzled round and stared down into my helmet.

The good news was, he hadn't done a poo. The bad news was, he'd done a wee.

The unKeelest wee ever

The worst thing about your little brother doing a wee into your brand new SHNOZINATOR 9000 before you've even managed to charge it up is that WEE COMPERLEETERLY BREAKS A SHNOZINATOR 9000.

'Oh Barry,' said my mum, cuddling me into her dressing gown for the second time that morning.

me inside dressing gown

I wriggled out of my mum's dressing gown and looked at the little green triangle on the side of the helmet. It flickered, turned red, then fizzled out.

'Can you fix it, Dad?' I whimpered, feeling like a little light had fizzled out inside my belly.

32

'Hmmm, not sure I can Barry,' said my dad, peering into the SHNOZINATOR 9000. His face peered back up at him, reflected in the pool of wee.

'Can we take it back to Feeko's then?' I said. 'We could swap it for one that hasn't got wee all in it!'

My dad looked at me the way I look at my best friend Bunky when I feel sorry for how tiny his brain is.

'I don't think Feeko's takes back SHNOZINATOR 9000s that've been weed into, Barry,' he said.

I stood still for a trillisecond as I tried to work out what to do.

Desmond was sitting on the sofa watching the telly with a grin on his face. Lying on the carpet was his cuddly Clowny Wowny, also doing a grin.

sort of scary looking

My brain cells started to boil like
a kettle.

I walked over to Clowny Wowny and
trod on its stupid belly. Then I bent
down, grabbed its head and gave it
a tug.

Here is a fact about cuddly Clowny
Wownys you might not know: **their
heads rip off much easier than
you'd think.**

'Waaahhh!' screamed Desmond
Loser the Second as I dropped Clowny
Wowny's head into my SHNOZINATOR
9000 full of wee and stomped upstairs
to bed.

The end
(of chapter)

The great birthday telling-off

'Barry Garry Larry Loser, what DO you think you are doing?' said my mum, swinging my bedroom door open.

'I'm having a bday nap,' I said.

'Don't act clever with me, young man. I mean downstairs,' said my mum, her eyebrows tilting into their angry positions.

'Ooh, now let me think,' I said. 'I believe I was ripping Clowny Wowny's head off and dunking it in his owner's wee.'

Saying it out loud like that made me sound like a bit of a weirdo. I grabbed a pillow and squodged it over my head, wishing it was a SHNOZINATOR 9000 that'd zap me straight to Shnozville.

cloud head

'I know you're upset about your Shnozi-whatsitcalled, but that doesn't mean you can go around breaking other people's things!' shouted my mum.

'But he broke my thing first!' I screamed.

'I don't care,' said my mum, grabbing my arm and marching me down the stairs again. 'Desmond's a baby - he doesn't know what he's doing. You're a big boy, Barry - you should know better!'

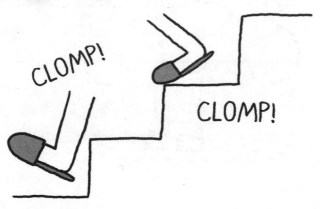

CLOMP!

CLOMP!

'It's my birthday! I don't HAVE to know better!' I cried. 'Can we go to Feeko's, Mum? Pleeease can we get me another SHNOZINATOR 9000?'

'We most certainly cannot - I'm not made of money, you know!' said my mum. 'Now apologise to your little brother.'

my mum made out of money

'Sorry I ripped Clowny Wowny's head off, even though you weed into my SHNOZINATOR 9000,' I grumbled.

Desmond, who'd comperleeterly
forgotten about Clowny Wowny,
remembered Clowny Wowny and
started to scream again.

'And you'll be sewing that head back
on as soon as it comes out of the
washing machine!' my mum said to me.

excuse me
while I do
a massive
yawn

'Ooh, what a brillikeels bday I'm having!'
I said, flomping down on the sofa.

My dad did one of his funny faces
to try and make me laugh.

not
funny
at all

'Why don't you play with your other
presents?' he said, stuffing one of
Desmond's nappies into my
SHNOZINATOR 9000 to soak up
the wee.

'Oh what, like my boring old Wolf
Tizzler book?' I mumbled.
My mum looked sad for a
billisecond, and I felt a bit bad.

'You could at least have a look,'
she said. 'Wolf Tizzler's a very clever
young man - you might learn something!'

'Oh I'm SO sorry your loserish, big-nosed
son isn't all perfect like your darling
Wolf Tizzler!' I cried.

that nose
I mentioned

'Don't be silly Barry, you know
you'll always be my number one
Snookyflumps!' cooed my mum.
'Anyway, it's not like your Shnozi-
whatsit's working so you may as
well give it a go.'

She passed me the book and plodded
off into the kitchen to make a cup
of tea. 'Stupid rectangular cuboid,' I
said, opening it up and starting to read.

like what
you're doing
right now

HOW TO
BE A
GENIUS
LIKE ME

And to my surpriseypoos it
immedikeely gave me one of my
brilliant and amazekeel ideas.

Yellow jumper

'Happy birthkeels to you!' sang my best friends Bunky and Nancy Verkenwerken two hours, eighteen minutes and thirty-six seconds later, when I opened the front door and saw them standing there.

'Did you get a SHNOZINATOR 9000?'
grinned Bunky. 'Is it the keelest thing
in the whole wide world amen? Why
aren't you wearing it right now? If I
had a SHNOZINATOR 9000 I'd put it on
and never take it off again for the
rest of my life!'

Bunky
(sort of
like a dog)

I took a deep breath and opened
my mouth.

'Desmond Loser the Second used it as a potty so I ripped Clowny Wowny's head off and dunked it in the wee,' I said. 'I just sewed his head back on. Back to front.'

Nancy and Bunky gasped.

Nancy

'I am SO sorry, Barry,' said Bunky, leaning forwards and giving me a hug, which was weird. I don't think Bunky's ever given me a hug before.

'Don't worry about it,' I said, wriggling out of his weirdo hug. 'I'm comperleeterly over it.'

'That's good,' said Nancy, giving me a funny look because the last time something bad like that happened to me, it took about nine years for me to recover.

under duvet for whole time

'Nice polo neck, by the way!' she smiled. 'You look like Wolf Tizzler!'

Bunky looked at my polo neck and scratched his bum. 'Erm, what're you doing with your yellow hoodie?' he said.

'I'll put it back on later,' I said. 'I'm only wearing this because it's my bday jumper.'

'Can I wear it then?' said Bunky. 'Your yellow hoodie, I mean?'

I've always had the feeling Bunky secretly wanted my yellow hoodie, just from the way he looked at it. Now I knew I'd been right all along.

Bunky's dream

'Er, no-o?' I said. 'Get your OWN yellow hoodie!'

'I would if I could,' said Bunky. 'But my mum keeps on buying these stupid stripy ones!' He pointed down at his stripy jumper. It was true, I'd never seen him wearing anything else.

every
single
day →

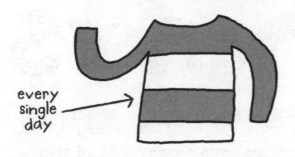

'Tough luck, Stripy,' I said. 'Nobody wears Barry Loserkeel's yellow hoodie - apart from Barry Loserkeel!'

Bunky stomped his foot on the ground. 'My name isn't Stripy!' he cried, as Nancy pointed at my book.

'Er, what are you doing with that?' she said.

Bad news

'It's my new Wolf Tizzler book,' I said, holding it up so they could read the title. 'I've just been reading it!'

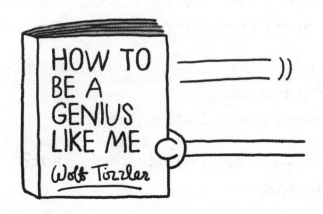

HOW TO BE A GENIUS LIKE ME
Wolf Tizzler

'You read a BOOK?' said Bunky, screwing his face up like used wrapping paper.

spotty!

'Well, the first chapter . . .' I said.

'What in the keelnees did you do THAT for?' said Bunky.

'I know, it's weird,' I said. 'And what's even weirderer is I'm actukeely quite enjoying it!'

Nancy rolled her eyes like a two-wheeled sellotape dispenser. 'Shock horror!' she chuckled.

too weird?

'Bunky, Nancy, I've got some bad news,' I said, comperleeterly out of the blue.

Nancy's eyebrows tilted into their worried positions. 'What is it, Barry? Are you OK?'

'Sorry, did I say BAD news? I meant GOOD!' I smiled. 'I was just trying to get your attention - it's one of Wolf Tizzler's tricks!'

Barry Tizzler

I held up the page in HOW TO BE A GENIUS LIKE ME where Wolf Tizzler talks about saying things like 'I've got some bad news' to make people's ears prick up.

'So what's your news?' asked Nancy.

'I'm becoming an inventor!' I said, pulling at the neck of my polo neck.

I don't know if you've ever worn a polo neck before, but it really clings to your neck.

clingsville

'An inventor? What for?' said Bunky, already beginning to look bored. That's the thing with people like Bunky who've got tiny brains - they can't concentrate on things for more than three sentences.

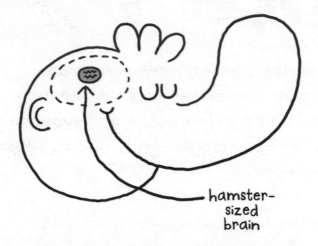

hamster-
sized
brain

'Let me fill you in while we take a stroll,' I said, tucking my book under one arm and my bright pink piggy bank under the other.

Bday Barry

'Coo-wee, Bar-ry!' cried my mum, running out of the house after us. 'Don't forget I've got your favourite dinner for tonight - fish fingers, chips and peas!'

I gave my mum a thumbs-up, not wanting to tell her that that hasn't been my favourite for about three years. 'Brillikeels!' I shouted over my shoulder, just to keep her happy.

'Nice piggy bank, Barry!' laughed Bunky as we strolled up the street. 'It goes with your girl's phone!'

I pulled my phone, which is pink and used to be my mum's, out of my pocket.

flower sticker on it too

'Why does everyone think pink is for girls?' I said. 'Some of the keelest things in the whole wide world are pink!'

'Like what?' said Bunky.

'Erm . . . bubble gum, strawberry milkshakes . . . the insides of eyelids?' I said, running out of keel pink things pret-ter-ly quick-er-ly.

bubble gum

insides of eyelids

strawberry milkshake

'Ooh, the insides of eyelids, they are SOOOO keel!' laughed Bunky.

I pressed a button on my phone.
'PLEUUURRRFFF!' it rumbled, doing a
blowoff right into his face.

Bunky's
face
over
here

'POOWEE!' sniggled Bunky, even though
the noise hadn't smelled of anything.
It was just this keel little app I'd
downloaded that's got millions of
different blowoff noises on it.

'Er, I don't want to interrupt your important discussion about eyelids and blowoffs, but what exactly are we doing?' said Nancy.

'Yeah Barry,' said Bunky. 'Since when do you take STROLLS?'

'It's something Wolf Tizzler does,' I said, tapping my book. 'It helps him think clearly!'

'Ugh, Wolf Tizzler . . .' sighed Bunky. 'My mum thinks he's the best thing since sliced bread!'

what's the big deal?

I chuckled to myself, wondering who invented sliced bread, then remembered I'd forgotten to mention something important.

'Let's clear one thing up before we go any further,' I said.

'Yeah yeah, we know!' smiled Nancy, nudging Bunky, and he pretended to fall off the kerb into the road and down a drain.

'What?!'

I said.

'Today's your birthday, which means you're "Bday Barry", which means you can do whatever you like and we can't say anything about it!' said Nancy.

'How did you know that?' I grinned.

'Because you say it EVERY birthday!' laughed Bunky.

I did a bday sniggle and we all strolled along for about seven and a half footsteps. 'What I don't get,' said Nancy, 'is why aren't you more upset about your SHNOZINATOR 9000 being weed into?'

I smiled to myself all mysteriously, mostly because that's what Wolf Tizzler says you should do on page seventeen of his book. It makes people think you've got something interestikeels to say.

'The reason is this,' I said, stopping still suddenly and shooting my hands up in the air. 'I'm gonna become a billionaire and buy myself a new one!'

A bird cheeped in a tree, sounding a bit like it was doing a 'TA-DA!'

'Barry Loser, a billionaire?' laughed Bunky. 'How in the name of unkeelness is that ever gonna happen?'

billionaire Barry

'Easy! I just have to come up with an invention like the ZOOM-E-BROOM!' I said. 'How hard can it be?'

'Very?' said Nancy.

I put my hands on Nancy's shoulders and stared into her eyes, which is something Wolf Tizzler says you should do to make people concentrate on what you're saying. 'Nancy, Nancy, Nancy,' I smiled. 'How long have we known each other?'

'Too long,' said Nancy.

CLIP
CLOP

'Exactly!' I said. 'And you still don't realise? I'm a child genius, Nancy - just like Wolf Tizzler! Do you know how many brilliant and amazekeel ideas I've had?!'

Bunky started counting on his fingers. 'He's right, Nancy. Barry's had a LOT of brilliant and amazekeel ideas.'

'There's a difference between CALLING your ideas "brilliant and amazekeel" and them actually BEING brilliant and amazekeel,' said Nancy.

Bunky did his confused face, which is just his normal face.

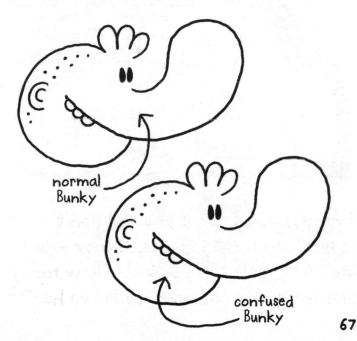

normal
Bunky

confused
Bunky

'Look, we can all stand here wasting our time talking about whether I'm a child genius or not,' I said, pulling at the neck of my polo neck*. 'Or we can just agree that I AM one and get on with making a billion pounds!'

Nancy chuckled to herself. 'Come on then, Bday Barry,' she said. 'I'm in!'

scratching his bum
↓

*The neck of my polo neck really was clinging to my neck.

The Slugbusters

I opened HOW TO BE A GENIUS LIKE ME to page twelve and started reading out loud. 'The first job of being an inventor is to find a problem to solve,' I said.

Nancy took her glasses off and cleaned them on her jumper. 'Hmmm, we need a problem to solve . . . WAAAHHH!!! SLUG!!!'

'Hey, don't call me Waaahhh Slug!' I said. Then I looked down at Nancy's shoe and saw a slug slithering across it like a slimy zombie eyebrow.

'There's another one!' cried Bunky, pointing at another slug, sitting on a leaf that was sticking out of a tree next to my head.

'IT'S AN INVASION!' I screamed, pretending to run off like **Future Ratboy** in my favourite **Future Ratboy** episode, 'Future Ratboy and the invasion of the Nom Noms'.

OUT NOW!

Nancy plucked the slug off her shoe and plopped it down in the front garden we were standing next to.

The lawn was covered in millions of big fat slugs, chomping on the grass.

'I've heard about this – it's something to do with the unseasonably warm winter we just had,' said Nancy, peering through her glasses at the lawn. 'The slugs didn't hibernate – they just kept eating and getting fatter and having more babies!'

'How do you know all this stuff?' said Bunky, peeking into Nancy's earhole to get a look at her brain.

'The Mogden Gazette!' said Nancy. 'Don't you read newspapers?'

Me and Bunky laughed. 'Er, no, Nancy, I don't read newspapers!' he said.

because we're not old grandads

'Anyway, back to me becoming a billionaire,' I said, walking in the direction of Mogden High Street. 'We need to find a problem to solve!'

Two old grannies were walking towards us at minus seven millimetres per hour. 'Ooh, these slugs are a menace, Ermentrude!' warbled the one on the right, who had moles dotted all over her face like squidgy brown full stops.

SHUFFLE
SHUFFLE

'Tell me about it, Gladys,' said Ermentrude. She was bent over in half so that her face faced the floor, which must've made it easier for her to spot slugs. 'They're 'aving a field day wiv me Begonias!'

'Ooh, me begonias!' warbled Bunky, doing an impression of Ermentrude, and we all sniggled.

granny
Bunky

'Ooh, me Begonias!' I warbled as well, and Bunky and Nancy stopped sniggling. 'Oi, why aren't you laughing?' I said, pulling at the neck of my polo neck again.

'Sorry Barry, your voices just aren't as funny as Bunky's,' said Nancy, and Bunky nodded, looking all pleased with himself.

The old grannies waddled off round the corner and Nancy blinked. Not that she hadn't been blinking anyway. 'Hang on a millikeels, I think I've got it!' she said.

'Got what, slug-shoe-itis?!' sniggled Bunky, putting his hand up for me to high five, but I just ignored him.

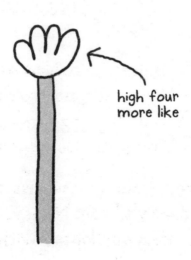

high four
more like

'What is it, Nancy?' I said, even though I really should've been in a mood with her for saying my voices weren't as funny as Bunky's.

'The slugs - if we could come up with an invention that got rid of all the slugs in everyone's gardens we'd be billionaires!'

Slug pellets

'I don't want to ruin your bday party or anything, but you have heard of slug pellets, right?' said Bunky, and Nancy and me stopped doing the little dance we'd been doing.

'ARGH! Slug pellets!' I cried, dropping to my knees. 'Why did someone have to invent slug pellets?!'

Nancy smiled down at me, which was a funny thing to do seeing as her brilliant and amazekeel idea had just been comperleeterly ruined.

'What's so funny?' I said, getting up and dusting off my trousypoos.

'Oh, just that there aren't any slug pellets left in the whole of Mogden!' grinned Nancy.

'No slug pellets? In the whole of Mogden?' I said.

'They've all sold out!' said Nancy.

'Sold out? I gasped.

'Oh my keelness Barry, could you stop repeating everything Nancy says?' said Bunky.

'Stop repeating everything Nancy says?' I said, and Bunky sniggled.

'It was on the front page of the Mogden Gazette!' said Nancy.

Bunky pretended to stroke an invisible beard. 'Well, I MUST read the Mogden Gazette more often, it sounds absokeely FASCINATING!' he said, doing an old grandad voice.

MUNCH

CHOMP

And that's when I heard a non-old grandad voice.

Ooh la la

'Ooh la la, if eet eesn't my leetle friend Barry Loser!' it said, and I looked around.

'Renard!' I smiled, spotting my French friend Renard Dupont lying on a sun lounger in his front garden. At least I think it was his front garden.

'What crazee plan eez eet you are up to zees time, Barry?' chuckled Renard, walking up to us and leaning over his fence.

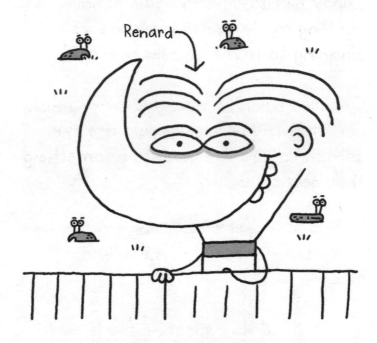

Renard

'It's my birthday!' I said, high-fiving Renard. 'I'm gonna become a billionaire and buy a SHNOZINATOR 9000!'

Bunky looked at my hand and stomped his foot. 'Hey, you just IGNORED my high five!' he said.

"Appy birfday, Barry!' said Renard, ruffling my hair. 'And 'ow are you planning to make all zees money?'

I pointed behind him at his lawn, which was crawling with slugs just like the garden before. 'By inventing something that gets rid of THOSE!'

logo for invention

Just then, Renard's front door opened and his mum walked out. 'Mama, zees eez my leetle friend Barry Loser,' said Renard.

'Bonjour, Madame Dupont!' I said, showing off that I knew how to say 'hello' in French.

"Allo, Barry!' said Madame Dupont, and I introduced her to Bunky and Nancy.

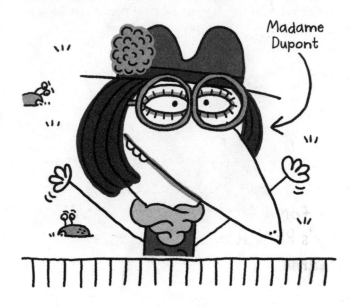

Madame Dupont

'Bunkee?' said Madame Dupont, kissing him on both cheeks, which is how French people shake hands. 'Zees eez une unusual name, non?'

'Funny you should say that, Madame Dupont,' I smiled, because I happen to know for a fact that 'Bunky' isn't Bunky's REAL name, it's just his nickname.

Bunky gave me a nudge. 'Did you know we were inventors, Madame Dupont?' he said, comperleeterly changing the subject, because he HATES people knowing his real name.

Renard pointed at the slugs. 'Zey are getting rid of ze slugs for money, Mama!' he grinned.

'Ooh la la! Zees eez ze answer to my prayers!' cried Madame Dupont. 'I 'ave been down to Feeko's, but zey 'ad none of ze pellets left!

sold out

FEEKO'S SLUG PELLETS

'That's why I've invented the SLUG-ZAPPER 5000!' I said, making up what I was saying on the spot.

Nancy leaned over to me and whispered. 'What in the name of keelness is the SLUG-ZAPPER 5000?'

'Just go with it,' I whispered, remembering what it said on page fifteen of Wolf Tizzler's book:

Don't worry if you haven't got an invention yet. The name is the most important part.

15

Madame Dupont pushed her glasses on to her forehead and looked me in the eyes. "Ow much eez zees SLUG-ZAPPER fingy goin' to cost me?' she said.

'1p per slug!' barked Bunky before I could even open my mouth.

Bunky dog

1p per slug

'Eet eez une deal!' said Madame Dupont, walking back into her house. 'Just do not 'urt my precious snails!'

'1p per slug?!' I cried, turning round to Bunky. 'Let Bday Barry do the talking next time, "Bunky".'

Bunky ignored me and turned to Renard. 'What's your mum talking about, "don't hurt my snails"?' he said.

Renard bent down, scrabbled around in the grass and popped back up holding a snail between two of his French fingers. 'Yum yum!' he said. 'In France we are eating ze snails!'

day ruined →

'Yum yum?!' said Bunky. 'Are you comperleeterly crazy?'

'Absokeely non, Bunkee,' said Renard.
'Ze snail eez une delicious fing!'
He rubbed his tummy, plopping the
snail back on the ground.

I watched the snail slither underneath
a leaf and thought back to when I
had a pet snail once called Snailypoos.

But that's another story.

in all keel
bookshops!

Barry
Loser

I am so over
being a Loser

Snailypoos

'So, the SLUG-ZAPPER 5000 eh, Barry?'
said Nancy, and I shrugged.

'It got us the job, didn't it?' I smiled,
leaning against a tree. 'Now all we
have to do is come up with a brilliant
and amazekeel invention that'll get rid
of all these slugs!'

'How about if we just pick them
up and put them in a box?' said Bunky,
and I de-leaned against the tree and
whipped Wolf Tizzler's book out from
under my arm, flipping it open to
page twenty-nine. 'Sometimes the best
invention is the most obvious,' I read
out loud.

'What, so your invention is your HAND?' said Nancy, looking down at my bday hand like it was just an ordinary non-bday one.

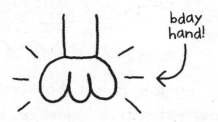

bday hand!

I Future-Ratboy-darted my eyes around Renard's garden and spotted a scratched-up old ice cream tub with a stack of those sticks you write the name of plants on inside it.

'Let's just see how many we can collect!' I said, grabbing the tub and bending over to start making some money.

A nice sit-down

It was forty-seven minutes and fifteen seconds later and the ice cream tub was full.

'That's the garden cleared. How many slugs have we got?' said Bunky, and I passed the tub to Nancy, who everyone knows is the fastest at counting slugs.

'A hundred and seventy-eight!' she said a hundred and seventy-nine seconds later, which is actukeely pretty slow for her.

'Wowzers, we're rich!' grinned Bunky.

'Woop-de-poo-poos, one pound seventy-eight,' I said, doing my sarcastic voice. 'Not exactly gonna buy me a SHNOZINATOR 9000 is it?'

worst bday
pressie ever

'Let us take a stroll,' said Renard, who'd been lying on his sun lounger for the most of the slug-picking-up bit, reading Wolf Tizzler's book.

still loads left

'Good idea, Renard!' I said, and we all strolled to Mogden High Street, where we stopped strolling and looked around for somewhere to have a nice sit-down.

'Cafe Cafe?' said Bunky, pointing to Cafe Cafe which is his favourite place to have a nice sit-down at the moment, mostly because the waiter who works there used to babysit him when he was a little kiddywinkle.

Cafe
Cafe

CAFE CAFE

Cafe Cafe

'Bunky my brother!' grinned Herman the waiter as we walked through the door of Cafe Cafe. It was dark inside and full of grown-ups sitting in front of their laptops drinking coffees.

Bunky walked up to Herman and gave him a high five, then looked back at me to see if I was jealous. 'A Fronkle for everyone. We're rich, Herman!' he said.

Herman

'Er, we're not rich yet, Bunky,' said Nancy, pointing at my bright pink piggy bank with the £1.78 Madame Dupont had given us inside it.

'Don't worry, they're on the house!' said Herman. 'Me and The Bunkmeister go way back!'

Herman disappeared behind the bar
and we sat down at a little table next
to a man with a ginormous beard and
a comperleeterly bald head.

'Pssstt, Barry!' whispered Renard. 'Zees
man, ee looks like 'is 'ead eez on upside-
down, non?'

I glanced over at the man and did
a sniggle, and the man tutted and
carried on tapping away on his laptop.

'So now what, Mr Genius?' said Nancy, as Herman walked over with a tray of Fronkles. 'We've got £1.78 and a tub full of slugs.'

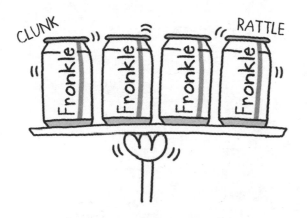

She pointed at the ice cream tub, which I'd plonked down on the table. The lid was on and inside squirmed a hundred and seventy-eight juicy fat slugs.

'Well we can't carry on collecting slugs,' I said. 'I mean, what are we sposed to do with THESE?'

'Maybe Renard could eat them?' said Bunky, and Renard shook his head.

'Do not talk crazee, Bunkee!' he said. 'I am only eating zee snails.'

snail, chips and peas

And that was when I noticed a familikeels-shaped head turning round in the darkness at the back of the coffee shop.

Fronkle-ccino

'Is that . . .' I said. 'It isn't, is it? It can't be . . .'

'The one and only,' burped Darren Darrenofski, the annoying little Fronkle-slurper from my class at school.

I don't know why I was so surprised to see him, actukeely. He's in there all the time.

'Nice piggy bank, Loser - same colour as my mum's favourite lipstick!' he cackled.

I pulled my phone out of my pocket, pressed a button and it did a big sloppy blowoff right in the direction of his nostrils.

Darren pretended to ignore the blowoff. He was sitting at a table by himself with an empty chair in front of him. 'Take a seat,' he said, pointing to the chair, and he picked up a tiny coffee cup and took a sip.

'Are you drinking COFFEE?' I gasped.
I was gasping because my mum NEVER
lets me drink coffee, even though her
and my dad drink about nine hundred
cups a day.

'Fronkleccino,' said Darren, holding up
the little cup. 'Can I buy you one?'

'Why would I want to have a
"Fronkleccino" with you?' I said,
remembering all the times he'd been
horrible to me at school.

ring pull thrown
at nose

bin over
head

using hood as
cereal bowl

My eyes were getting used to the dark, and I Future-Ratboy-zoomed them in on a big book that was sitting on Darren's table. HOW TO BE A GENIUS LIKE ME, said the words on its spine.

'You're reading Wolf Tizzler's book too?!' I cried, pulling at my polo neck.

I was beginning to regret putting the polo neck on, what with all the neck-pulling I was having to do.

over it

'Maybe I am, maybe I'm not,' said Darren, doing a blowoff into his chair and pointing at my tub full of slugs. 'I see you've got a problem . . .'

'What if I have?' I said.

'Maybe old Dazza can help you with it, that's what!' snarfled Darren.

'OK Dazza, we're listening,' said Bunky, comperleeterly butting into my business meeting with Darren, and I stomped on his foot under the table.

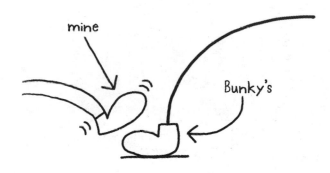
mine

Bunky's

'OK Dazza, I'm listening,' I said, as Darren pulled a toothpick out of a little pot on the table and stuck it between his teeth.

Nancy gasped. 'You're not going to toothpick them all to death are you?' she said.

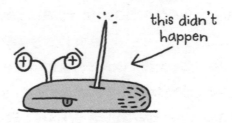

this didn't happen

'Relax,' smiled Darren. 'That's not my style!'

'So what IS your style then, Bogienose?' said Nancy, and Darren stopped smiling and checked he didn't have any bogies hanging out of his nostrils.

'How much did you get for those slime-sticks?' he said, nodding at the tub of slugs.

'1p each!' grinned Bunky, slurping on his can of Fronkle and I stomped on his foot again.

'Shush, Bunky! You're ruining my deal!' I whispered, and I twizzled my head round to face Darren's. '10p each,' I said, my left eye twitching. My left eye always twitches when I lie.

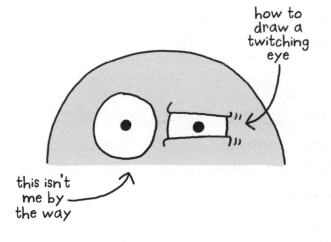

how to draw a twitching eye

this isn't me by the way

'I'll give you 2p,' smiled Darren.

'2p for the whole tub? What are you, comperleeterly crazy?' spluttered Bunky.

'I fink ee means 2p per slug, Bunkee,' said Renard, and Bunky did a face like even HE thought his brain might be a bit tiny.

same tops

'5p,' I said. 'And that's my final offer.'

'2p,' smiled Darren, and I stomped my foot, this time not on Bunky's.

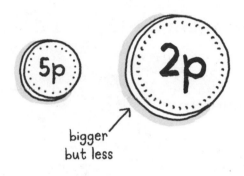

bigger but less

I looked at Nancy. 'It's double the money,' she shrugged.

'What you gonna do with them, Darrenofski?' I said, stroking the tub's lid and thinking of my old pal Snailypoos. 'I don't want any violence . . .'

'Trust me, Loser,' grinned Darren, stuffing his hand into his pocket and pulling out a fistful of dirty old 2ps. 'I'll make sure they go to a loving home.'

'Well in that case,' I said, 'you've got yourself a deal!'

Enter Sharonella

Darren waddled out carrying the tub of slugs and I rattled my piggy bank, which now had £5.34 inside.

'Still nowhere near enough for a SHNOZINATOR 9000,' I grumbled.

'What's that about you having a big shnoz, Bday Boy?' said a screechy voice, and I looked up to see Sharonella from my class walking through the front door of Cafe Cafe. 'Come 'ere, ya big Loser!' she cackled, giving me a great big squelchy smacker on the nose.

Shaz

'Eurgh, get off me!' I cried, grabbing a napkin from the dispenser on the table and wiping my bday nose dry.

Bunky gave me a look that looked like he was checking if he could tell her what we were doing, and I nodded.

'Guess what, Shazza – we're inventors!' he said. 'And we're gonna be billionaires too!'

'Oh gawd, not more Wolf Tizzler wannabes,' moaned Sharonella, waving to Herman. 'Scuse me honey, can I getta Fronkle over here?'

CLICK!

'Not WANT-TO-BES,' I said, tapping my piggy bank. 'ARE-A-BES! We've just gotta come up with an invention . . .'

Nancy rolled up her sleeves and grabbed a napkin from the dispenser. She pulled a pen out of her pocket and tapped it against her teeth. 'Let's brainstorm!' she said.

'Brainstorm?' said Renard. 'What eez zees terrible weather inside of your brain, Nancee?'

Nancy chuckled. 'A brainstorm is when you come up with loads of ideas all in one go,' she explained.

'So we can find an invention that'll make us billionaires!' grinned Bunky.

Herman handed Sharonella her Fronkle and I stood up, which is what I do when I want to get the keelness out of somewhere.

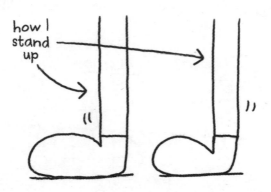

how I stand up

'Let's brainstorm, losers!' I said, heading for the door.

Really bad brainstorm

'Erm . . .' I ermed, staring up at the clouds as we strolled down Mogden High Street.

'Ummm . . .' ummed Sharonella, slurping on her Fronkle.

'Hmmm . . .' hmmed Nancy.

'Hey, I've got it!' said Bunky, clicking his fingers, and we all stopped. 'Nope, it's gone . . .'

I opened HOW TO BE A GENIUS LIKE ME to page thirty-eight and started reading out loud. 'Often the solution is right in front of your eyes . . .'

Bunky stared straight ahead. 'All I can see is air!' he said. 'And I can't even SEE it. It's useless! Let's just give up and be poor . . .'

air

'Don't be a loser, Bunky!' I said, at the exact same millisecond my nose bonked into something lamp-posty. 'OOF!' I blurted, rubbing my nose. 'Who put that lamp post there?'

A fluffy little black dog trotted up and cocked his leg, doing a wee against the lamp post's base, and the smell wafted up my nostrils.

remember for later

'POOWEE!' I cried. 'That's the third time I've smelt someone's wee today, and only one of those someones was me!'

The door of the sunglasses shop we were standing outside of swung open and the owner stepped out. 'Shoo, you little mutt!' shouted the man, who was wearing bright green triangle-shaped sunglasses. 'Blooming dogs always weeing up my lamppost,' he grumbled, reversing back into his shop.

want

SSES

I looked down at the wee-soaked lamp post, then up through the window at the grumpy shop keeper. Then I thought back to my dad earlier that morning, stuffing one of Desmond's nappies into my SHNOZINATOR 9000.

'Oh my unkeelness!' I cried, giving myself a back-to-front salute. 'I think I've cracked it!'

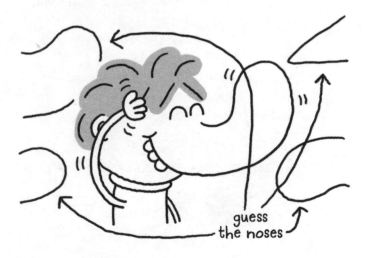

guess the noses

Lamp post nappies

'Lamp post nappies?' said Nancy once
I'd explained my invention to them all,
which was this:

Inside-out nappies
taped round the base
of lampposts to soak
up dog wee.

Nancy pushed her glasses up her nose.
'That's it, I'm out!' she said, starting to
walk back in the direction of her house.

'Where are you going?' I cried, running
after her and doing my Wolf Tizzler
shoulder-grab thing. 'Nancy, Nancy,
Nancy, how long have we known each
other?' I said, staring into her eyes.
'Remember, this is Bday Barry's day!'

'Look, "Bday Barry",' she said, staring back at me. 'I'm all up for helping you get a new SHNOZINATOR 9000, but if I'm going to do it, I'm going to do it properly.'

'Meaning?' I said.

stuffed piggy bank and book in pockets

'Meaning we have to come up with an invention that's got a chance of actukeely making us some money!' she cried.

I turned round to face the rest of my bday gang.

'She eez correct, my leetle friend,' said Renard. 'Zees lamp post nappy idea - eet eez really, really bad.'

that's weird

'OK,' I said, doing a bday sigh. 'Let's go back to the drawing board.'

Back to the drawing board

'Which way's this drawing board thingy then?' said Bunky, looking left and right.

'It's just a phrase, Bunky,' I said as we started to stroll. 'Now, who's got an idea?'

'Ooh, me, me!' said Sharonella, waggling her hand in the air. 'Fake leaves!'

'Fake leaves?' said Renard.

'Fake leaves!' grinned Sharonella. 'Like when it's winter and all the leaves on your trees have fallen off - you could buy fake leaves to stick on the twigs!'

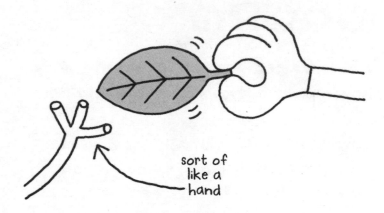

sort of like a hand

'NEXT!' sighed Nancy as we turned a corner and I almost bonked my bday nose into another lamp post.

This lamp post had one of those LOST DOG posters stuck on it, with a faded photo of a fluffy white dog called Fred in the middle.

looks familikeels

'Hey, isn't that the dog that just weed all over the grumpy sunglasses man's lamp post?' said Bunky, pointing at the photo.

'Spoiler alert - that dog was BLACK!' I said, peeking into Bunky's earhole and seeing right out the other side.

He clicked his fingers. 'I've got it - Toe Socks!'

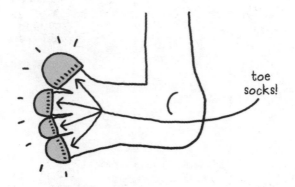

toe socks!

'Eurf, this is useless!' I cried, flipping open my book and reading out one of Wolf Tizzler's tips.

'Invent something that you'd want to buy yourself.'

I peered into my brain, trying to see if there was anything I needed.

kind of keel with no hair

Apart from the SHNOZINATOR 9000, my life was pretty keel. I had a nice enough mum and dad, and my baby brother Des wasn't that bad as long as I ignored him.

'What else do I want?' I wondered out loud, and I remembered the present list I'd stuck on the fridge door nineteen and three-quarter weeks before:

1. Another yellow hoodie

2. No more boring questions about school

3. A SHNOZINATOR 9000!!!

'Oh my unkeelness!' I cried. 'I want number two!'

Bday poo

'Hey everybody, Bday Barry needs a poo!' cried Bunky in his stupid granny voice, and they all did a sniggle.

'That's not what I meant!' I said.

'There's a toilet in Feeko's up the road!' said Bunky, grabbing my arm. 'Hurry Bday Barry, I'll get you there before you do your number two!'

DRAG

I wriggled out of Bunky's grip and prepared to do one of my funniest voices ever. 'Relax Bunky baby, I don't need a poo!' I said, sort of mixing **Future Ratboy's** voice in with one of those old grannies from earlier.

'I am sorry Bday Barry, but zees voice you do, eet eez not funny een ze slightest,' said Renard.

I pulled at the neck of my polo neck and started to explain about my present list and how 'number two' on it was 'No more boring questions about school'.

'Let me get this straight,' said Nancy once I'd finished. 'Your invention would be some kind of gadget that can answer boring old mum-and-dad questions so the kids don't have to?'

"O"

hovers next to head maybe?

I nodded, thinking how I actukeely DID kind of need a poo all of a sudden, probably because Bunky had just mentioned it.

'That's not bad,' said Nancy, and everyone else nodded.

'See, told you I was a child genius!' I said, waddling towards the Feeko's Supermarket at the end of the road, blowoffs seeping out of my bum. 'Stupid blowoff app must be broken!' I said, blaming them on my phone.

'How's it gonna work tho, Bazzy?' said Sharonella as the doors to Feeko's slid open and we headed towards the toilets at the back. "S'not exactly like you can just magic up some machine wot answers any old question, is it?'

We were walking down the Electronics aisle and I stared up at the SHNOZINATOR 9000 shelves, thinking how I'd probably be back in here in about two days' time, buying a brand new one with my billions of pounds.

got!

gelled-back hair

suitcase of cash

SHNOZ-INATOR 9000

SHNOZ-INATOR 9000

'LAST FEW LEFT!' shouted a sign hanging above the last three helmets. 'FACTORY COMPLETELY SOLD OUT!'

'GAAAHHH!!! We've got to hurry!' I screeched, waddle-zooming towards the toilet to do my bday poo.

Loo-serish idea

'Eez zat better, Barry?' said Renard as I walked back out of the toilet.

'Much better thanks, Renard,' I said, holding my bday hand up for a high five, but he just shook his head.

Sharonella stomped on my foot to get my attention. 'As I was saying, how's this invention of yours gonna work?'

'Good question, Shazza,' I said, letting her off the foot-stomp seeing as I was in a hurry what with all the SHNOZINATOR 9000s almost being sold out. 'It just so happens I had one of my brilliant and amazekeel ideas when I was sitting on the loo!' I smiled.

'That's where I get ALL my best ideas!' grinned Bunky, giving himself a mini-salute.

'Two words . . .' I said, and the whole gang stared at me, waiting to hear what they were.

stop looking at me

Hi brow

'"Hi brow"?' said Nancy, saying the two words I'd just said. 'Isn't that that thing **Future Ratboy** puts on his forehead in "**Future Ratboy** and the annoyingness of the really annoying neighbour"?'

'Exackeely, Nancy! Well done!' I said, doing my hands-on-her-shoulders thing, and she stomped on my bday foot.

The 'Hi brow' is this keel little extra eyebrow that **Future Ratboy** sticks on to his forehead in the episode where he's got an annoying new neighbour who keeps asking really boring questions.

Instead of **Future Ratboy** having to keep on answering the questions, the Hi brow does it for him.

Yes it is a lovely day isn't it

three
nostrils

I pulled my pink phone out and typed
in the website for **Future Ratboy**, then
clicked on the page where it explains
about all his keel little gadgets.

'The Hi brow consists of a simple circuit
board, a fake eyebrow and some glue
to attach it to the user's forehead,'
I read out loud.

'And where are we gonna get all
that stuff?' said Bunky.

'Follow me,' I said, walking towards
the Women's Beauty aisle.

Down the Women's Beauty aisle

"Ow eez eet zat you know where zees zings are, Barry?' said Renard as I reached up and grabbed a packet of stick-on fake eyebrows off the shelf.

'My Granny buys them,' I said, walking towards the checkout. 'She burnt her real ones off putting her face too close to an electric fire when she was a kid!'

stuck on

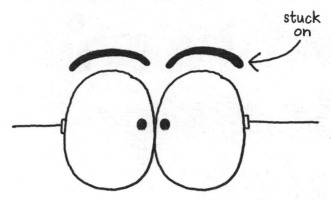

'That's what happens when you haven't got a TV,' said Bunky, all seriously.

I stepped up to the checkout. 'That'll be £3.49 please love,' said the lady behind the counter, whose name tag said 'Delia'.

I jangled my piggy bank upside-down until £3.49 chinked into my hand. 'That leaves £1.85,' said Nancy.

Delia

'Oof, how're we gonna afford a whole circuit board with that?' said Bunky, and I twirled around.

'Don't you worry about that, Bunky baby! I got one of those build-your-own circuit board kits for my bday,' I said, handing the £3.49 to Delia.

Frozen goods, I mean bads

'STOP!' cried Nancy, and we all froze like fish fingers on a frozen goods aisle.

'What eez eet, Nancee?' said Renard, his mouth moving while the rest of him stayed still.

'It's this stupid Hi brow invention!' said
Nancy. 'I don't want to ruin it for
everyone, but . . . it's just not gonna
work!'

I held up the bag of stick-on eyebrows
and waggled them in her face.
'Er, hello-o?' I said.

'Barry, that **Future Ratboy** website's
just for fun. You can't actually make
a real-life Hi brow by attaching some
stupid little circuit board to a stick-on
eyebrow!'

I looked round at the rest of the gang as they thought about what Nancy had said. 'Nancy's right, Bazza,' said Sharonella, and they all nodded, Delia included.

like those nodding dog things

'Oh, what a surprise ...' I said, handing the eyebrows back to Delia, and she passed me my £3.49. 'Nancy thinks my bday idea is rubbish!'

'I don't think the IDEA's rubbish,' said Nancy. 'Just the invention. You need something more realistic!'

'Realistic my bum,' I said, pulling my phone out and blowing it off in her face.

PARP!

'That's not very nice, Barry,' said Delia, calling me by my name even though we'd only just met and I wasn't wearing a name tag. 'Say sorry to Nancy.'

'Sorry, Nancy,' I said, pulling at the neck of my polo neck. But Nancy just stared at my phone and smiled.

Nancy's idea

'What's so funny, Nancy?' said
Delia, who was beginning to get on
my nerves.

'Barry's phone!' said Nancy, clicking
her fingers. 'Why didn't I think of it
before!'

Bunky looked at me and itched his
bum. 'What's she talking about,
Bazza?' he said.

'Yeah Nance, what are you talking about?' I asked.

Nancy pointed at my phone. 'How much did you pay for that blowing off app thing?' she said.

'50p?' I said. 'No, a pound!' I added, remembering how I'd paid extra for the 'Super Sloppy' - a three-minute-long blowoff that was worth every penny I'd begged my mum to give me for it.

no head $\longrightarrow$

'You see - mobile phones are where all the money is these days!' said Nancy. 'What if we turn Barry's idea into an app?'

Bunky scratched his nose with the same finger he'd just scratched his bum with. 'How do you make an app out of a fake eyebrow?' he said.

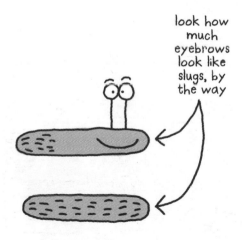

look how much eyebrows look like slugs, by the way

Nancy rolled her eyeballs. 'No-oo!
I mean an app that answers all the
boring questions mums and dads ask
about your day at school!' she smiled.

'What, like Bazza's blow-off fingy
except wiv words insteada blowoffs?'
said Sharonella.

'Exactly, Shaz!' said Nancy. 'Barry, you're good at coming up with horrible little things to say - all we need is a few of those and Bunky could do the voices for them!' said Nancy.

'Yeah, Bunky's well good at voices!' giggled Sharonella, and Renard did a snortle.

'Zees could be a real, 'ow you say, "money spinnurr", non?' he grinned.

I pulled at the neck of my polo neck and wondered if it was getting hot in Feeko's or if it was just me. 'Whoa, whoa, whoa, let's just calm down for a billisecond,' I said. 'If anyone's doing the voices for this thing it's ME!'

Sharonella looked at Nancy, who looked at Renard, who looked at Bunky, who looked at Delia, who looked at me.

me down here

'I really do think Bunky's the person for the job, Barry,' she said.

'OK, OK,' I sighed, seeing as we were running out of time to buy a SHNOZINATOR 9000. 'But Bday Barry's in charge!'

The parent-shutter-upper-er seven trillion

'Right. First things first. We need a name for this app!' I said, clapping my hands together so everyone would look at me.

I nicked that trick off page thirty-three of Wolf Tizzler's book, by the way.

'Erm . . . how about THE BUNKY-
NATOR NINE BILLION?' grinned Bunky.

I gave Bunky that tiny brain
look I was talking about earlier.

'It's got to explain what the app
actually does . . .' said Nancy.

'THE PARENT SHUTTER-UPPER-ER?' said
Sharonella, and I looked at
everyone's face apart from Delia's.

NO
DELIAS!

'I like zees!' said Renard.

'Me too!' grinned Bunky.

'It's not bad . . .' mumbled Nancy.

'I don't know, it needs a little something extra . . .' I said.

pepper?

'How about THE PARENT SHUTTER-UPPER-ER SEVEN TRILLION?' said Delia.

'Delia's cracked it!' I cried, partly because Delia HAD cracked it, but also because I just wanted to get the unkeelness out of Feeko's.

Naughty Bunky

'Let's go back to my house!' I said, heading towards the exit. 'We can record Bunky's voices in my room!'

'Whoa, whoa, whoa!' cried Bunky, copying what I'd said three minutes earlier. 'I can't just do my voices at the drop of a hat, Barry!'

'You 'ave dropped your 'at, Bunkee?' said Renard, looking around on the floor. 'But I deedn't see an 'at on your 'ead ...'

Bunky just ignored him. 'I haven't even had lunch yet,' he warbled. 'I'm starrrving!'

Bunky peered at the rack of chocolate bars next to Delia's checkout and grabbed two, one for each of his brain cells. 'I'll take these please, Delia!' he said. 'Barry'll pay.'

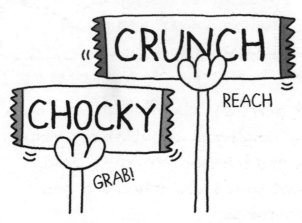

"CRUNCH

REACH

CHOCKY

GRAB!

'Oh he will, will he?' I said, reminding myself of my dad.

Nancy gave me a nudge. 'Just buy him the chocolate bars, Barry,' she said, reminding me of my mum.

'Well, don't eat them all at once then,' I said, jangling £1.29 out of my piggy bank and handing it over to Delia, because that's how much the two bars came to.

The worst walk home ever

'Come on then, Bazza,' said Sharonella as we walked back to my house, Bunky eating both of his chocolate bars at once. 'You gonna come up wiv some of your 'orrible little sayings for this app fingy or what?'

Nancy scratched her head. 'They've got to be answers to the most common questions mums and dads ask about school,' she said. 'Like, "What did you do at school today?" for example.'

'Eurgh, my mum ALWAYS asks me that!' groaned Bunky.

not that lost dog from earlier

'What did you do at school today, Barry?' said Nancy, trying to get me to come up with one of my brilliant and amazekeel answers.

← too many noses?

'Erm, answer boring questions?' I said, saying what I'd said to my mum earlier that morning, and everyone sniggled.

'That's not bad, actually!' smiled
Nancy. 'Now Bunky, you say what
Barry said, but in one of your
funny voices!'

'Gotcha!' grinned Bunky, spluttering
bits of chocolate all over the
pavement.

chocolate
rain

'What did you do at school today, Bunky?' said Nancy.

'Derm, danswer doring destions?' said Bunky in his blocked-up-nose voice, and Nancy, Sharonella and Renard all cracked up.

'Oh my days Bunky, you make me LARF!' cackled Sharonella, zigzagging all over the pavement and bumping into me by accident.

I bumped back into Sharonella
accidentally on purpose. 'Derm, dexcuse
me, dut I was de one who came up wid
dat!' I said in MY blocked-up-nose voice.

Nobody cracked up.

tough
crowd

'OK, moving on,' said Nancy. 'Barry,
how was Maths today?'

I carried on walking, pretending I hadn't heard her. There was no way I was going to answer her stupid questions if nobody was gonna crack up at my hilarikeel bday voices.

'Come on, Bday Barry!' said Nancy. 'How was Maths?!'

'Yawnsville times rubbish, divided by unkeelness,' I said.

you do
the maths

'Barry eez une natural at zees, non?' sniggled Renard.

'I've gotta hand it to ya Bazza,' said Sharonella, 'that ain't half bad.'

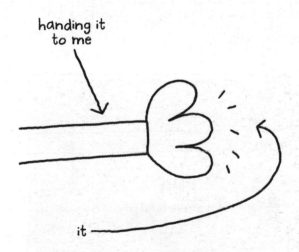

handing it to me

it

Nancy looked at Bunky and raised her eyebrows. 'Maybe in your granny voice?' she said.

'Ooh, yawnsville times rubbish, dear. Divided by unkeelness!' warbled Bunky.

'Ooh la la!' cried Renard, leaning on Sharonella to keep himself from falling over. 'Zees voices, zey are keeling me, Bunkee!'

starting to get on my nerves

'Ooh la la, my name eez Renard and I love Bunkee!' I said in my French voice, and I pulled at the neck of my polo neck to get a bit of air down into my jumper.

NNNGGGFFF!!!

'What's that sposed to be Bazza, Welsh or something?' giggled Sharonella, and Renard started cracking up again.

'All right, all right, we've got two answers to boring questions. I reckon one more and we can start recording,' said Nancy. 'How about, "What did you have for lunch?"'

'Er, fooood?' droned Bunky in the voice he does when he's pretending to be someone really boring.

'HAAA HA HAAAAAA!!!' cried Sharonella, her legs giving way, and she collapsed to the ground.

TEE HEE HEE!

'Hang on a millikeels,' I said. 'I thought Bday Barry wrote the lines!'

I peered down at Sharonella, then up at Renard, who was wiping tears away from his eyes. Nancy had taken her glasses off and was leaning against a lamp post, shaking with laughter.

HA HA HA!

lamp post is like, what's so funny?

'Oh forget it, let's just get this app up for sale so I can buy my SHNOZINATOR 9000,' I said, turning the corner on to my road. 'The sooner I zap myself to Shnozville the better!'

Back at the Loser residence

'Helloooo Barry's friends!' said my dad, opening the front door and giving me a bday hair-ruffle.

'Bonjour! Eet eez une pleasure to meet you, Monsieur Loserre. My name eez Renard Dupont!' said Renard, kissing my dad on both cheeks.

'Er yes, very nice to meet you Bernard,' said my dad, backing away into the living room.

blushing, not make-up

'Ooh, what a charming young man!' cooed my mum, carrying a basket of washing into the kitchen, and Renard kissed her on the cheeks too.

'Oh, so I'm number THREE on your list of favourite sons now am I?' I said. 'Wolf Tizzler, Renard Dupont, then rubbish old Barry the Loser!'

My mum gave Nancy a look that said, 'Typical Barry!' and Nancy gave my mum the same look back.

'I saw those looks,' I said. 'Bday Barry sees everything!'

Just then Desmond waddled into the hallway holding Clowny Wowny with his head sewed on back to front. 'Me love you, Bawwy!' he beamed, but I just ignored him and started stomping upstairs.

STOMP!
STOMP!
STOMP!

Sharonella turned to my mum.
'Oi, guess wot we're up to,
Madame Loser.'

'Come on, Shazza!' I boomed,
already halfway up the stairs.

stopping
stomping

'Ooh, I don't know, Sharon!' said my
mum, stuffing her giant red dressing
gown into the washing machine.

remember
this

'Bunky's doing his funny voices for an app fingy we're gonna sell for billions of pounds,' said Sharonella, and my mum smiled.

'That sounds like fun!' she said. 'Bunky's ever so funny with his voices.'

I leaned over the banister and opened my mouth extra wide. 'Why don't you do your impression of my mum, Bunky?' I shouted, and Bunky's face went all red like my mum's dressing gown.

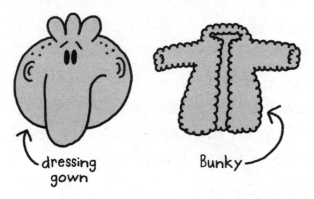

dressing gown

Bunky

'Ha ha, Barry's only joking,' said Bunky, and he bounded up the stairs followed by Nancy, Sharonella and Renard.

'I've got Barry's favourite tonight - fish fingers, chips and peas!' yelled my mum after them. 'You're welcome to join us!'

sorry
Renard

'That's not my favourite any more,' I grumbled to myself, propping my phone up on my homework desk and opening the microphone app.

Bunky. Or should I say...

Bunky sat down on my homework chair and rolled his shoulders a few times. He cleared his throat and combed his hand through his hair.

'And . . . ACTION!' I said, pressing RECORD on my phone.

Bunky took a deep breath. Then let it out again.

'What in the unkeelness are you doing?' I whispered. 'We're running out of time, Bunky. Feeko's has only got a few more SHNOZINATOR 9000s left, and the factory's comperleeterly sold out!'

Bunky leaned forward and pressed PAUSE. 'Don't pressure me, Barry. I don't need this pressure.'

talking to
my phone

'Pressure?!' I laughed. 'What pressure? Just do your stupid voices!'

Sharonella nudged Renard. 'Look Rennie, they're having one of their lovers' tiffs!' she sniggled.

'Put a sock in it, Shazza!' I shouted, picking one of my dirty rolled-up socks up off the carpet and throwing it at her mouth.

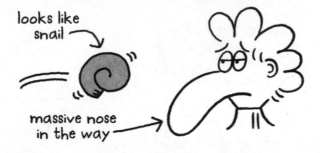

looks like snail

massive nose in the way

I turned back to Bunky. 'Are you gonna do this or not?' I said. 'Because if you're not, Bday Barry's more than happy to take over.'

Bunky leaned back in my homework chair and laughed. 'Oh per-lease!' he chuckled. 'You couldn't do it if your NOSE depended on it. Your voices aren't funny in the SLIGHT-ER-EST!'

'Watch it, Bunky,' I said. 'Remember, I'm the brains of this operation.'

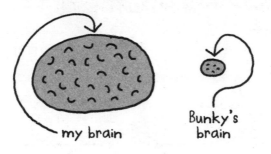

my brain

Bunky's brain

'Don't make me LARF, Barry!' chuckled Bunky. 'Anyone can think up a few stupid words. It's my funny voices that'll make people buy the app!'

'I'll tell you what makes ME larf, "Bunky"...' I said.

'What?' said Bunky.

'Your REAL name!' I boomed.

Bunky sat up straight, his eyes darting round the room. 'H-ha, ha, I-I don't know what you're talking about, Barry!' he stuttered.

'Let me remind you, then. I believe it begins with the letter "N"...' I said, swizzling Bunky's chair round with my foot.

SWISH!

'Wot you chatting about, Bazza?' said Sharonella, halfway through peeling a Not Bird sticker off my bedpost. 'Bunky's name begins wiv a B, dunnit?'

Not Bird (Future Ratboy's sidekick)

'Don't, Barry,' said Nancy, who's the only other person apart from me and Bunky's mum who knows his real name.

'Don't what?' I said. 'Tell everyone Bunky's real name?'

Renard looked at Nancy, then at Bunky, then at me. 'I really, really want to know zees real name of Bunkee's!' he said.

'Me too!' cackled Sharonella, sticking the Not Bird sticker on her top.

loads
still
left

Bunky got up off my chair. 'Seriously, Barry, if you do . . .' he said.

'If I do, WHAT?' I said.

Bunky looked down at me the way a dog looks at its owner when they're being mean. 'Don't worry, I'm not going to tell everyone your real name,' I said.

And then I shouted, 'NIGEL!!!'

Nigel V Snooky-flumps

'NIGEL?!' screeched Sharonella, flomping back on my bed, cackling with laughter.

'Knee gel?' said Renard, looking confused. 'Zis eez when you ave urt your knee and you need some gel to make it better, non?'

'NIGEL!' I shouted as Bunky, I mean
Nigel, stomped out of my bedroom.
I ran into the hallway and hung over
the banister. 'Come back, Nigel, I was
only joking!'

not
laughing

The front door slammed and I walked
back into my room.

'I hope you're proud of yourself, "Bday
Barry",' said Nancy, giving me her mum
stare.

'What?' I said. 'It's his name. What's
wrong with saying someone's name?'

'Barry?' called my mum up the stairs. 'Is everything all right, Snookyflumps? I think Bunky's just left!'

Renard scratched his head. 'Snooky flomps?' he said. 'Oo eez zees Snooky flomps when e eez at ome?'

thinking in French

Sharonella snuggled her head into my pillow and smiled up at the ceiling. 'Looks like old Snookyflumps has gone and ruined his chances at making a billion pounds!' she snortled.

'Oh why don't you go and do a great big smelly blowoff, Sharonella?' I said. 'As if I needed Bunky, I mean Nigel, to make a billion pounds. I can do funny voices JUST as well as he can!'

'No, you can't, Barry,' said Nancy, heading over to the door. 'I'm going to see if Bunky's all right. I hope you enjoy the rest of your birthday.'

selfish
or what

She slumped down the stairs and shut the front door behind her. 'Nancy's left, too!' shouted my mum from the kitchen.

I turned to Sharonella and Renard and pictured the last few SHNOZINATOR 9000s on the shelf in Feeko's. 'Anyone else think I can't do funny voices?' I boomed, in my hilarikeels old grandad voice.

funny or what

Sharonella and Renard looked at each other, then at the carpet.

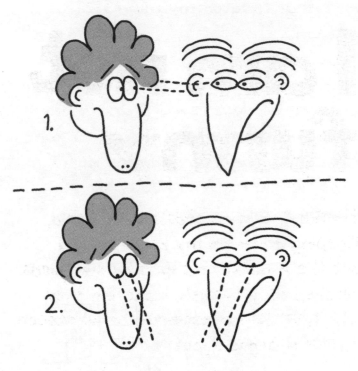

'Oh just go home,' I said, pointing at my door.

I am not funny

'Friends . . . who needs them?' I said, flopping down on my bed. I peered out the window and spotted two birds perched on a branch, bickering over who had the longest beak or whatever it is birds argue about.

My bedroom door creaked open and my mum poked her massive nose round it. 'Just thought I'd say, Sharon and Bernard have left as well,' she said. 'Everything all right, Barry?'

like a shark

'Fine,' I mumbled, and my mum
reversed her nose out of my room
and clomped back down the stairs,
her knees clicking on every step.

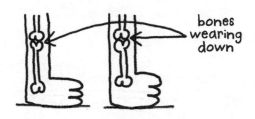

bones
wearing
down

I jumped up and went over to my
desk. 'We'll see who's the funny one!'
I said, pressing RECORD on my phone.

I took a deep breath and combed my
fingers through my hair. 'What did you
do at school today, Barry?' I said in my
normal voice, just to warm myself up.
'Derm, danswer doring destions?'
I answered in my funniest blocked-
up-nose voice.

'Ha ha! That's the hilarikeelest thing
I've heard in the whole entire history
of the universe amen!' I giggled, pressing
REWIND on my phone and then PLAY.

'What did you do at school today,
Barry?' droned a voice out of my
phone's speakers.

It didn't sound like me exactly.
It was a bit dronier than usual.

droney
Barry
(get it?)

'Derm, danswer doring destions?'
it droned again.

'Hmmm, must be something wrong with the microphone,' I muttered, giving the phone a tap on the table and pressing RECORD.

'Barry, how was Maths today?' I asked in my normal voice. 'Ooh, yawnsville times rubbish, dear. Divided by unkeelness!' I warble-replied.

granny
Barry

I pressed REWIND then PLAY.

'Barry, how was Maths today?' droned my voice. 'Ooh, yawnsville times rubbish, dear. Divided by unkeelness!'

'Oh,' I said, getting up from my desk and walking back to my bed. I sat down on the edge of it and sighed. 'No wonder my ex-friends didn't laugh at my funny voices,' I mumbled. 'They're not funny in the slighterest.'

still
bickering

Chat to Wolf!

I flomped back on my bed and grabbed
HOW TO BE A GENIUS LIKE ME off the
side table. I opened it up and slotted
it over my face like a book-shaped
SHNOZINATOR 9000.

'At least I'm still a child genius,' I said,
thinking how tiny Bunky's brain was.
'Who needs funny voices when you're
a billionaire inventor, anyway?'

'You OK, Snookyflumps?' called my mum up the stairs for the eight trillionth time. 'Dinner in five mins!'

'Yessss I'm fiiiine,' I droned in my boring, unfunny voice. But I wasn't fine at all. I was comperleeterly lonely.

Future Ratboy poster

'All on my bday own with nobody to talk to,' I grumbled. 'What a loseroid . . .'

And just as I was saying the word 'loseroid', the book slipped off my face. It donked on to my bed and slammed shut.

'Stupid rectangular cuboid,' I said, picking it back up and glancing at the back cover.

There was a photo of Wolf Tizzler next to the bar code at the bottom, with a speech bubble popping out of his grinning mouth. 'Chat to Wolf!' said the words inside the speech bubble.

get microscope
and read

Underneath the photo was the link for Wolf's website: www.WolfTizzler.com.

'Hmmm,' I hmmmed, pulling my phone out of my pocket and tapping the website into it. I clicked on the 'Chat to Wolf' button and a rectangle-shaped box appeared.

> Please enter your login details:

said the words inside it.

I made my username 'barry_winner' and my password 'b@rryisthekeelest!'

A little green bubble popped up and I typed 'Hello' into it.

Chat to Sunil

The words 'Hello barry_winner' appeared inside a little grey bubble, just underneath my green one.

I couldn't believe my unloserness. I was actukeely talking to the real-life Wolf Tizzler!

'Is that really the real-life WOLF TIZZLER?!' I typed, even though I knew it was.

'My name is Sunil. I will be your Customer Liaison Officer for this session,' said the words that appeared in the little grey bubble.

'Oh,' I said out loud. 'Oh,' I wrote into my bubble.

Sunil in here

'What can I help you with today, barry_winner?' typed Sunil.

'I spose I just wanted to talk to another inventor,' I typed. 'I'm a child genius like Wolf Tizzler, you see. Sometimes it can be a bit lonely...'

'Nice to meet you, fellow child genius!' typed Sunil.

'Do you have any advice for me?'' I typed. 'I'm trying to make a billion pounds so I can buy a SHNOZINATOR 9000. My baby brother weed in my one.'

Sunil's bubble stayed empty for a bit. 'Sorry to hear that, barry_winner. My advice is to focus on your goal. Stay true to your desires and work hard to make them real.'

I scratched my bum, which isn't an easy thing to do when you're already sitting on it.

'That sounds a bit boring,' I typed.

'Mr Tizzler believes that only boring people get bored,' typed Sunil.

'Oh,' I said out loud. 'But I get bored all the time,' I typed.

The only time I WASN'T comperleeterly bored was when I was with my friends, actukeely.

alone   not alone

'I think I might've been a bit horrible to my best friend Bunky,' I typed into my little green bubble. 'His real name's Nigel, and he doesn't like anyone knowing it, but I told Sharonella and Renard anyway. Cos they thought he could do funnier voices than me.'

Sunil's bubble stayed empty for a bit again. 'No offence barry_winner, but our algorithm is indicating that the probability of your being a child genius is minus seventeen per cent.'

'I. Don't. Even. Know. What. You. Are. Talking. About.' I typed.

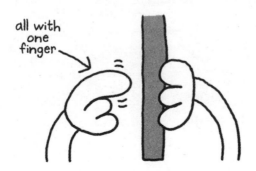

all with one finger

'My advice to you,' typed Sunil, 'is to make friends with your friend.'

I thought of Bunky, sitting somewhere all upset that everyone knew his name was Nigel. Then I thought of him doing his old granny voice, and I sniggled to myself.

not actukeely sitting

'Is that what Wolf would do?' I typed.

'Wolf Tizzler doesn't have time for things like friends,' typed Sunil.

I peered back out the window at the two little birds. They'd stopped bickering and were tearing a worm in half, sharing it for dinner.

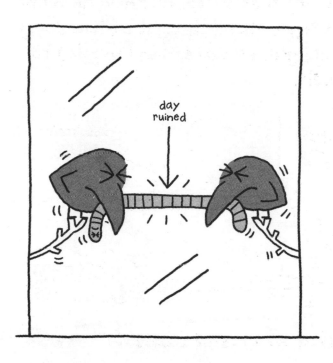

'K, thx bye,' I typed, stuffing my phone into my pocket and heading off to find Bunky.

Not my favourite

'Nancy's back, Snookyflumps!' cried my mum as I started donking down the stairs.

'What in the name of Shnozville are you doing here?' I said.

'Bunky's missing!' cried Nancy. 'I went looking for him but couldn't find him anywhere. His mum says he didn't come home for dinner!'

'Oh my unkeelness,' I said, pulling at the neck of my polo neck jumper. 'It's all my fault! I never should've told them his name was Nigel!'

My mum poked her nose round the kitchen door. 'You staying for Barry's birthday dinner, Nancy?' she smiled. 'It's his favourite - fish fingers, chips and peas!'

shark attack!

I put my hands on my mum's shoulders
and stared into her eyes, getting ready
to tell her fish fingers weren't my
favourite any more. 'Mumsy Wumsy,
I hate to break this to you, but . . .'

me down
here

'But what, Barry?' said my mum,
starting to look worried, and I
changed my mind.

'Back in a bday sec!' I cried, running
out the door.

Lost Bunky

'Where could he be?' said Nancy as we zoom-strolled down my road, me in the lead because it was my bday.

I turned the corner at the top and headed in the direction of Mogden High Street. 'I don't know, but we're gonna find out.'

A lamp post was growing out of the pavement like a leafless concrete tree. On it was stuck one of those LOST DOG posters we'd spotted earlier.

'Nancy, you still got that pen?' I said, clicking my fingers and holding out my hand.

Nancy fished around in her pocket and found her pen, dropping it into my palm. 'I might not be able to do funny voices,' I said, 'but I can still come up with genius ideas!'

I crossed out the word 'DOG' on the poster and wrote 'BUNKY' above it in capitals. Then I scribbled over the dog's ears and drew Bunky's three tufts of hair above its eyes. 'There!' I said, standing back.

The photo didn't look anything like Bunky. Not that it mattered, because I'd just spotted a familikeels silhouette out of the corner of my eye.

Too many Fronkleccinos

'What is it, Barry?' said Nancy,
following me across the road to
Cafe Cafe.

Inside it was comperleeterly dark
apart from one small light in the back
corner. The 'closed' sign was hanging on
the door and I squidged my face up to
the window, peering through.

looking through
two panes
of glass

'Why didn't I think of it before!'
I cried. Not that I'd been looking
for all that long. 'Of course he'd
come here!'

I banged on the door and Herman
wandered over, unlocking it and
letting me and Nancy in.

'He's in a bad way,' he said, leading
us through to the back. 'I tried to
find out what was wrong but he
wouldn't tell me. I think it's got
something to do with somebody
called Nigel?'

can't be
bothered
to explain

Bunky was slumped over Darren's table, empty Fronkleccino cups dotted around all over it. 'Too . . . many . . . Fronkleccinos . . .' he warbled.

'How many of those things has he had?' said Nancy, lifting Bunky's head off the table and leaning him back in his chair. 'Bunky, are you all right?' she said, and he did a Fronkleccino burp right into her face.

BURP!

'Bunky? Who's Bunky?' he whimpered, beginning to sob. 'I hate to break it to you Nance, but Bunky's DEAD!'

'Don't you ever say that!' I boomed, swiping the Fronkleccino cups off the table, and they crashed on to the floor. I think I was overdoing it a bit. Not that it mattered because it was my bday.

'Hey! Watch the crockery, man!' cried Herman, wandering off to get a dustpan and brush or whatever.

I pulled the spare chair out and sat down opposite Bunky. 'I'm sorry, Bunky,' I said, reaching over to hold his hand. Which was weird. I don't think I've ever held Bunky's hand before.

AWKWARD

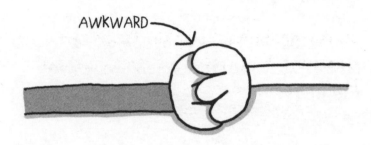

Bunky wriggled his hand out of mine and stared at me through his tears. 'It's too late for sorry,' he mumbled. 'Everyone knows my name is Nigel . . .'

'Not everyone!' I said, trying to make my voice sound un-droney. 'Only Shazza and Renard - and they won't tell anyone!'

It went quiet for a bit while we all tried to imagine Sharonella not telling anyone that Bunky's real name was Nigel on Monday morning at school.

'OK, Shazza might be a problem,' I said. 'But I'll deal with her.'

Bunky grabbed a napkin from the dispenser and wiped his eyes, just as Herman reappeared carrying a brand new ZOOM-E-BROOM.

like he's in an advert too

'You seen this thing in action?' he
smiled, sweeping up the plastic
Fronkleccino cups.

I glimpsed over at Bunky and did half
a smirk.

'Stupid Wolf Tizzler,' he snuffled,
blowing his nose and smirking the other
half back. 'I still haven't forgiven you,
you know,' he said.

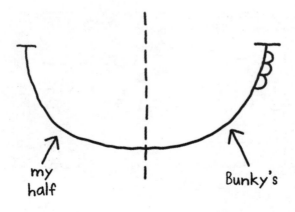

'Oh come on, Bunky,' I said. 'It's not like "Nigel" is even that bad a name. You wanna try "Barry Loser" out for size!'

Herman stopped sweeping and looked at Bunky. 'Your real name's Nigel?' he smiled, and Nancy stomped on his foot.

'That's between you and that lamp post outside!' she said.

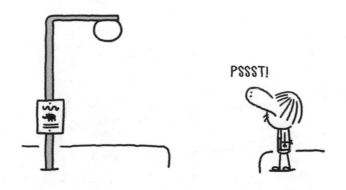

PSSST!

Bunky did a little chuckle and looked at my polo neck.

'I've got an idea for how you can pay me back,' he said, and I pulled at the neck of it, because it really did cling.

can you guess his idea?

Monday morning

It was Monday morning and me, Bunky and Nancy were strolling through the gates of Mogden School.

Sharonella wandered over to us with Renard, a ginormous smile on her face. 'Morning Barry, morning Nancy, morning . . . BUNKY!' she chuckled.

'Thanks, Shazza,' I said, rattling a 10p out of my piggy bank and handing it over to her for not saying 'Nigel'. 'How long's this gonna go on for, if you don't mind me asking?'

'Let's just say it'll be a while before you're a billionaire!' she cackled, dropping the coin into her pocket.

I thought back to my bday and shook my head. 'Oh I gave up on that idea DAYS ago,' I said. 'It was WAY too much trouble!'

'But what about zee SHNOZINATOR 9000, Barry?' said Renard. "Ow are you gonna afford eet now?'

where's he running?

'Feeko's sold out anyway,' I said. 'The last one went on Sunday afternoon...'

person who bought it

'I am SO sorry, Barry,' said Sharonella, leaning forward to give me a hug which I immedi-wriggled out of.

'Oh, I'm comperleeterly over it,' I said, looking round at them all. 'Who needs a SHNOZINATOR 9000 when I've got friends like you?'

'Really?' said Nancy.

not convinced

'Plus my mum and dad said they'd buy me one for Christmas!' I smiled.

'What about zat terreeble leetle brother of yours, Barry?' said Renard. "Ave you forgiven 'im yet?'

'Yeaaah,' I said. 'Desmond can't help it if he's a bit of a Loser sometimes!'

Sharonella pointed at my yellow hoodie. 'Nice yellow hoodie,' she said.

Not that I was the one wearing it – Bunky was.

dream come true

'Ooh, thank you, dear!' warbled Bunky in his old granny voice. 'It's mine all week – payback for young Barry here being such a naughty boy!'

Nancy did a sniggle. 'And I see your polo neck's had a little adventure too, Barry!' she said, pointing at my white jumper, which wasn't white any more, it was pink.

'Yeah,' I said, pulling at the neck of it. 'I threw it in the laundry with my mum's dressing gown by accident. Turns out you're not sposed to mix red and white clothes together in the washing machine.'

bad dream more like

'Ooh la la, 'ow do you not know zees, Barry?' chuckled Renard. 'Eet 'appens een every cheeldren's TV show I 'ave ever seen, non?'

Future Ratboy and the attack of the killer washing machines

Bunky ruffled my hair like he was my dad. 'Pink suits you, Bazza!' he laughed. 'It brings out the insides of your eyelids!'

Just then Anton Mildew from our
class ran past. 'Darren's here!' he cried.
'He's got a SHNOZINATOR 9000!'

Anton

'Huh?' I said, looking up. And that
was when I noticed something
unbelievakeel.

Super slug!

Darren Darrenofski was in the middle of the playground, a ginormous queue of kiddywinkles snaking off in front of him like a caterpillar. Slotted on to his piggy-shaped head was a SHNOZINATOR 9000 with the visor flipped up.

'How'd Darren afford a SHNOZINATOR 9000?' gasped Bunky as I Future-Ratboy-zoomed my eyes in on the queue.

All the kids were holding 10p coins in their hands. Next to Darren sat a humungaloid pyramid of tiny black cardboard packages.

They were all about the size of a
lipstick box and had the word 'SUPER
SLUG!' scribbled on the side of them in
red capital letters.

There was a yellow sticker on the lid
of each box with the words '10p ONLY!'
written on it.

'Our slugs, that's how!' I cried,
stomping over to him. 'Oi Dazza, you've
got some explaining to do!'

'Oh I have, have I, Loser?' snuffled Darren, taking 10p off the freckly-faced boy at the front of the queue and handing him a SUPER SLUG box.

drawing of what I just said

'Don't act all clever with me, young man,' I said. 'I've seen your little slug boxes. You think you can buy them off me for 2p each and sell them for 10?'

'I don't FINK I can,' said Darren.
'I KNOW it!'

Nancy tapped the freckly-faced boy
on his shoulder. 'Excuse me - can I have
a look at that, please?' she said, and
the boy thought for a second then
shrugged and handed it over.

'If you've done anything to hurt those
poor slugs . . .' said Nancy, staring at
Darren. She opened the lid and peered
into the box. Inside a slug was munching
happily on a bit of lettuce.

inside

'See - no violence,' burped Darren. 'Like I said, that's not my style!'

'How in the unkeelness did you get people to pay 10p for them?' said Bunky. 'They're just boring old slugs!'

'Page nineteen,' said Darren, pointing to the Wolf Tizzler book poking out of his rucksack. 'It's all in the packaging!'

Nancy handed the box back to the boy and he peered into it, doing a face like he'd just wasted 10p.

Renard stroked his chin and glanced down the queue at all the kiddywinkles holding their 10ps. 'But 'ow did you sell enuff of zees slug fingys to buy une SHNOZINATOR 9000?' he said. 'Zis gaming 'elmet, eet eez really, really expenseeve, non?'

Darren cackled to himself. 'Don't be stupid, Bernard!' he said. 'I didn't buy it with my slug money!'

slug money, get it?

'So ow DID you buy it then, Daz?' said Sharonella.

'I found that lost dog that's been on all the lamp posts!' he giggled. 'Barely recognised him at first - he was all black from dirt and stuff!'

'Black?' I said, remembering the little black dog that'd weed up against the moody sunglasses man's lamp post.

'Yeah, I gave him a wash and called the phone number on the poster,' grinned Darren. 'Nice big juicy fat reward - just enough for a SHNOZINATOR 9000!'

remember?

I watched the next kiddywinkle in
the queue as she handed Darren
her money.

Bunky tapped me on the shoulder.
'Er Barry? Spoiler alert - THAT WAS
THAT DOG WE SAW!' he cried.

does
actukeely
look like
the dog
a bit

But I just ignored him because I was
too busy coming up with one of my
brilliant and amazekeel ideas.

One last bday plan

Darren took the coin off the girl and held it up to his nostrils. 'Mmm, I love the smell of a 10p in the morning!' he snarfled, handing her a SUPER SLUG.

'Hmmm,' I said, giving my piggy bank
a little rattle and looking round at
my bday gang. 'Anyone thinking
what I'm thinking?'

don't
think so

'What you finking, Bazza?' said
Sharonella.

'Yeah Barry, what's your brilliant and
amazekeel idea this time?' said Bunky,
peering into my earhole.

I tapped Darren on the shoulder.
'What you want, Loser?' he burped.

'How much for a go on your
SHNOZINATOR 9000?' I said, and
he scratched his bum.

'The SHNOZINATOR 9000 is not for
sale,' he said, stroking it with the same
hand he'd just scratched his bum with.

putting me
off a bit

'Nice try, Bazza,' said Sharonella, patting me on the back, but I wasn't finished yet.

I whipped Darren's copy of HOW TO BE A GENIUS LIKE ME out of his rucksack and flipped it open to page fifty-nine. 'Everything has a price,' I said, reading out loud.

Darren smiled and peered at the piggy bank tucked under my arm. 'How much you got in that thing?' he said.

I held the piggy bank up in front of his face and gave it a rattle. 'Ooh ... enough for at least five goes, I reckon.'

Bunky started counting how many of us there were in the bday gang. 'Barry, Nancy, Shazza and Renard - that's four. So why do you want FIVE goes, Barry?'

'Hello?' said Sharonella, knocking on Bunky's forehead. 'Anyone ho-ome?'

KNOCK!

KNOCK!

'Oh yeah, and me!' giggled Bunky.

Darren snatched the piggy bank with his left hand and rattled it again.

'Ooh . . . that does sound luvverly,' he drooled.

Gordon Smugly from my class was the next person in the queue. 'Are you two going to stand around pretending to be Wolf Tizzler all day?' he sneered. 'Some of us have got SUPER SLUGS to buy!'

proper loser

Darren lifted the SHNOZINATOR 9000 off his head with his right hand and weighed it up against the piggy bank.

'COME ON!' cried a kiddywinkle from the back of the queue, and Darren smiled.

'Well?' I said, putting my arms round the bday gang, and we all took a deep breath.

'Looks like you've got yourself a deal, Loser!' said Darren, handing me the SHNOZINATOR 9000.

The end-inator!

(Apart from the next page)

About the author and drawer

Jim Smith is the keelest kids' book author and drawer in the whole world amen.

He graduated from art school with first-class honours (the best you can get) and went on to create the branding for a keel little chain of coffee shops.

He also designs cards and gifts under the name Waldo Pancake. And his favourite colour is pink.

Teacher breath in a cup!

← one of Jim's keel coffee cups